With gratitude and respect I dedicate this special edition of Little Red Riding Hood
to the people whose dream made the entire "Once Upon A Time" collection
a reality. Their unique vision continues to inspire me.

Tom Peterson   15 March 2002

Photographs © 1983 Sarah Moon
Published in 2002 by Creative Editions
123 South Broad Street, Mankato, MN 56001 USA
Creative Editions is an imprint of The Creative Company
Designed by Rita Marshall
Printed in Italy
Library of Congress Cataloging-in-Publication Data
Perrault, Charles, 1628-1703 [Petit Chaperon rouge. English]
Little Red Riding Hood / by Charles Perrault ; illustrated by Sarah Moon.
Summary: A little girl meets a hungry wolf in the forest while on
her way to visit her sick grandmother.
ISBN 1-56846-143-7
[1. Fairy tales. 2. Folklore--France.] I. Little Red Riding Hood. English. II. Title.
PZ8.P426 Li 2002   398.2'0944'02--dc21   [E]   2001053784

First Edition   5 4 3 2 1

LITTLE RED RIDING HOOD

Charles Perrault
ILLUSTRATED BY Sarah Moon

CREATIVE EDITIONS

MANKATO

Once upon a time

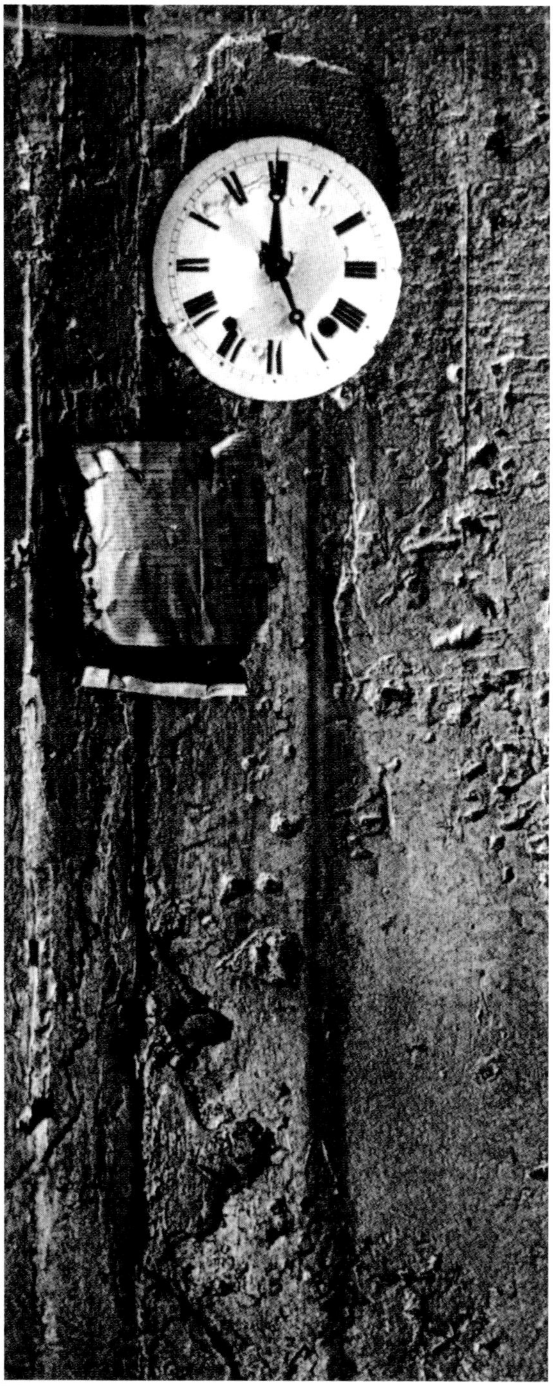

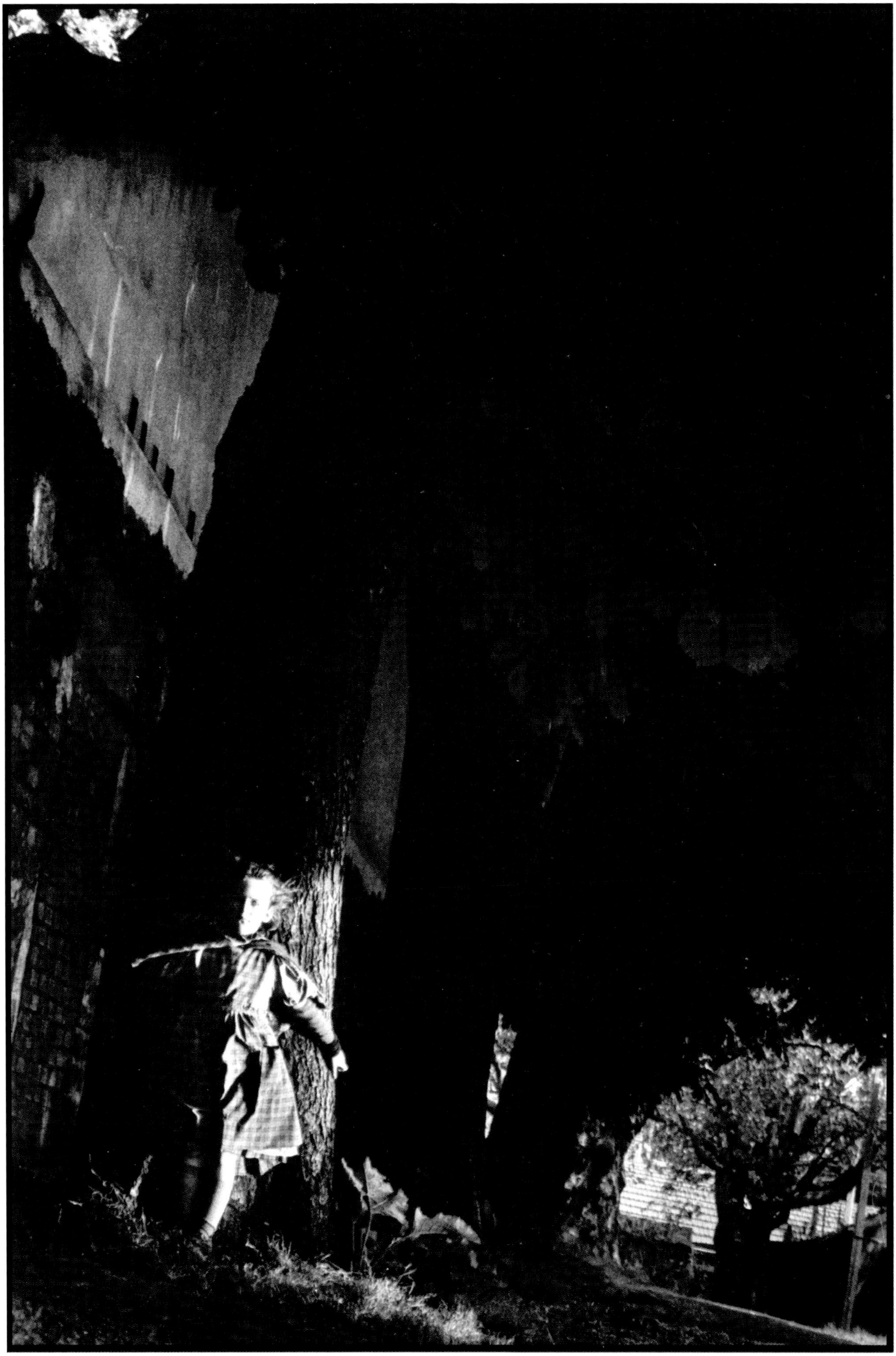

THERE lived in a certain village a little country girl, the prettiest creature who was ever seen. Her mother was excessively fond of her, and her grandmother doted on her still more. The loving mother made for her daughter a little red riding-hood. It was such a perfect and attractive fit that everybody called her Little Red Riding Hood.

One day her mother, having made some custards, said to her:

"Go, my dear, and see how your grandmamma is feeling, for I hear she has been ill. Bring her a custard and this little pot of butter."

Little Red Riding Hood set out immediately to visit her grandmother, who lived in another village.

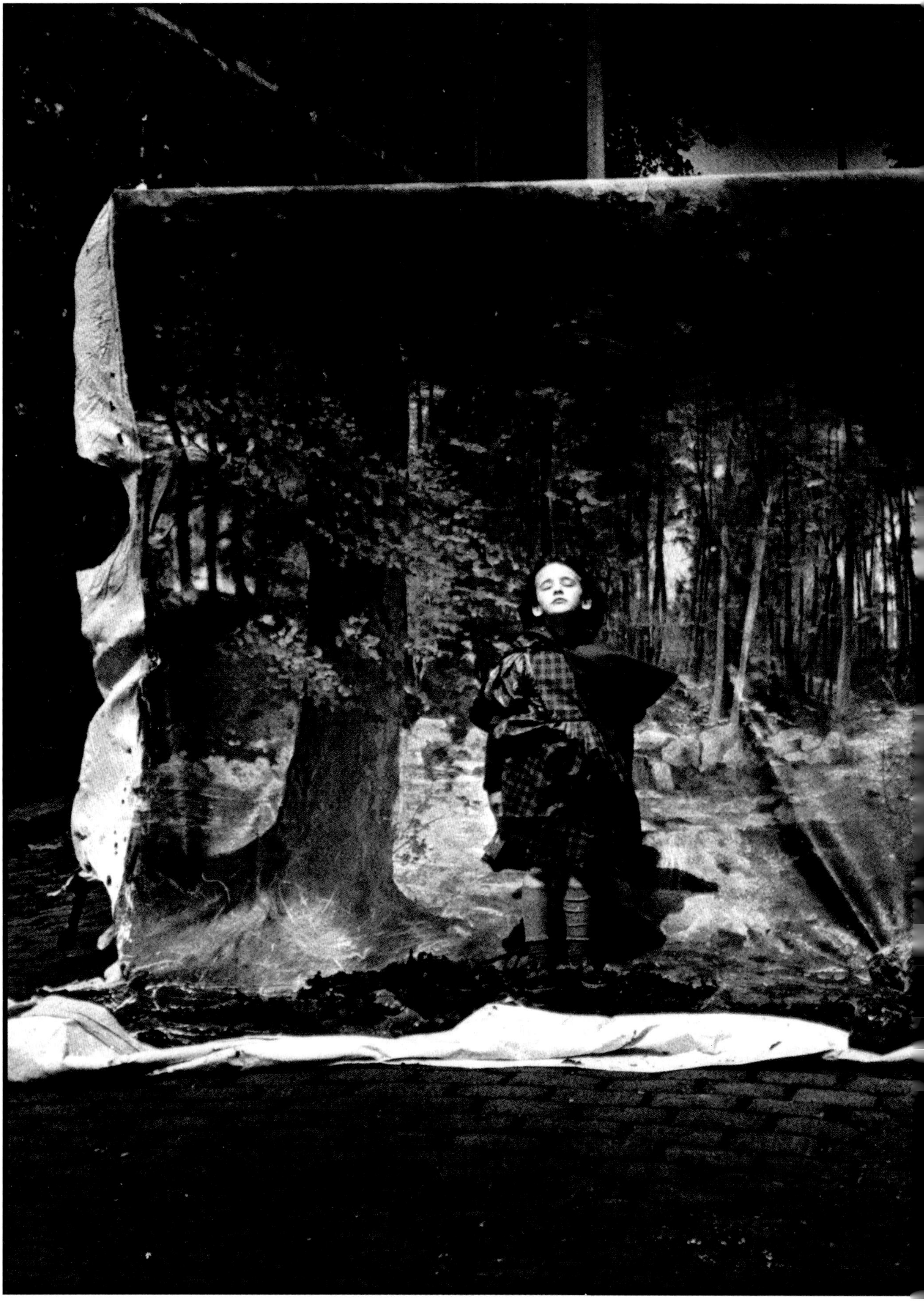

She was the prettiest creature who was ever seen.

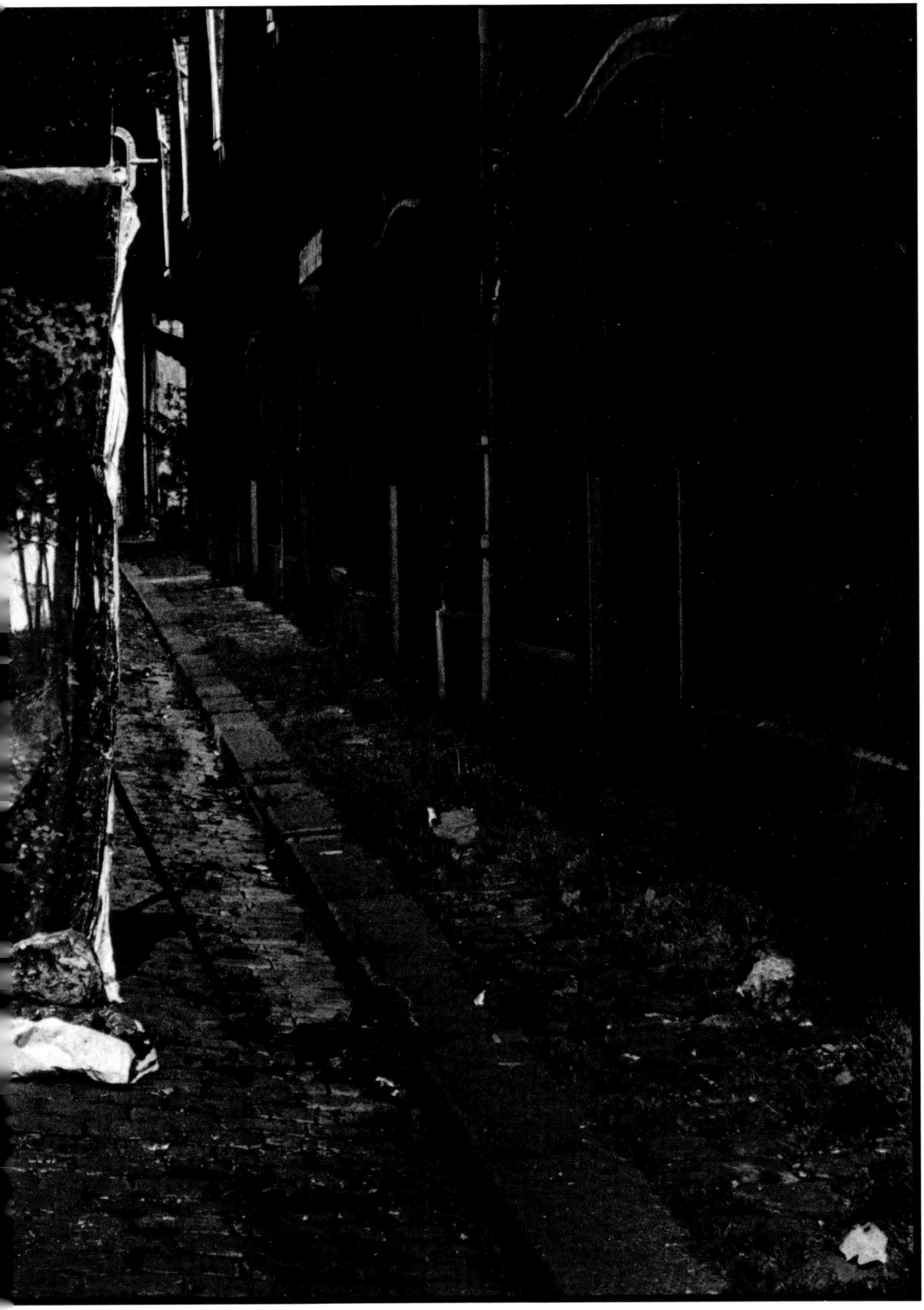

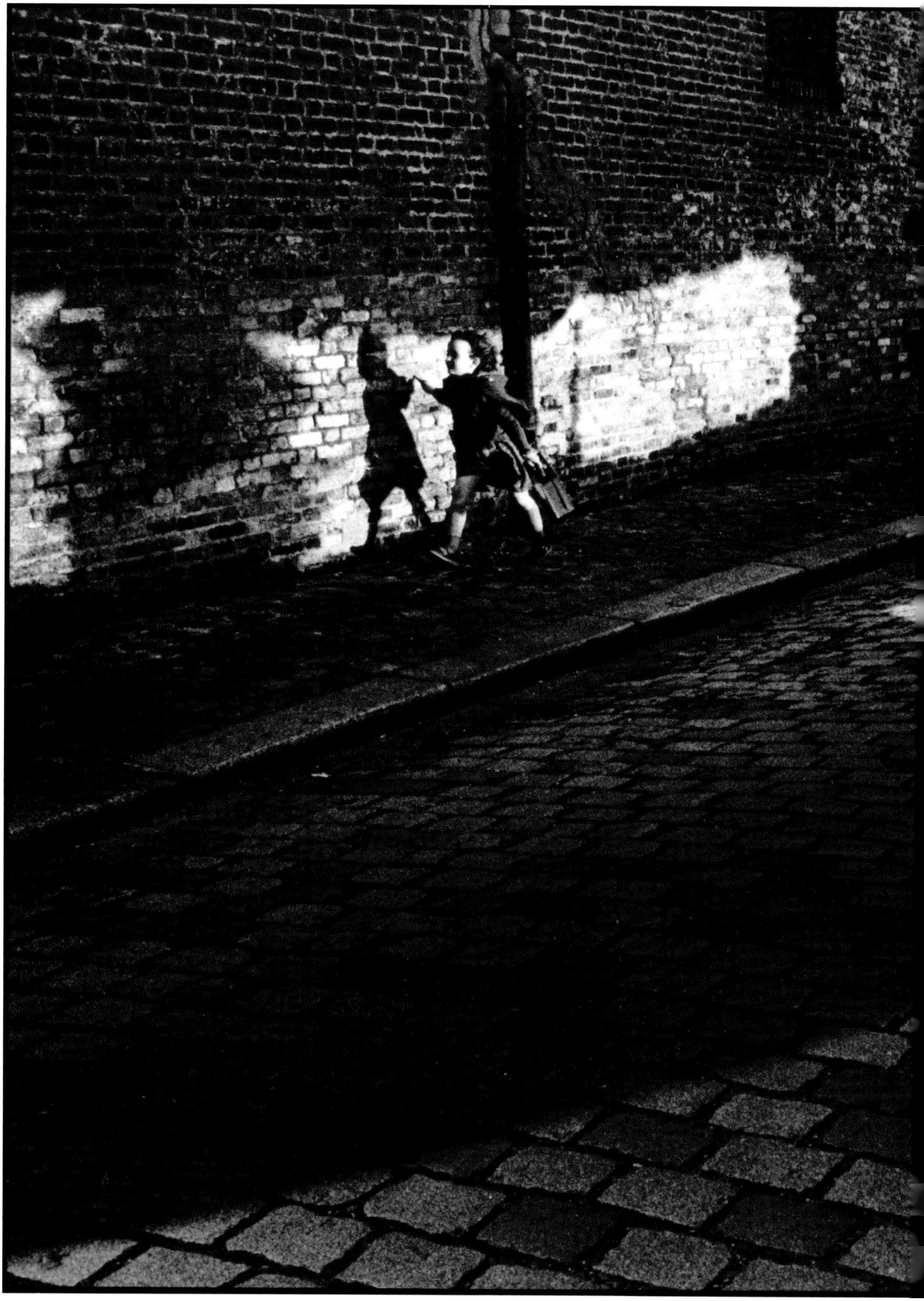

Little Red Riding Hood set out immediately to go to her grandmother's house.

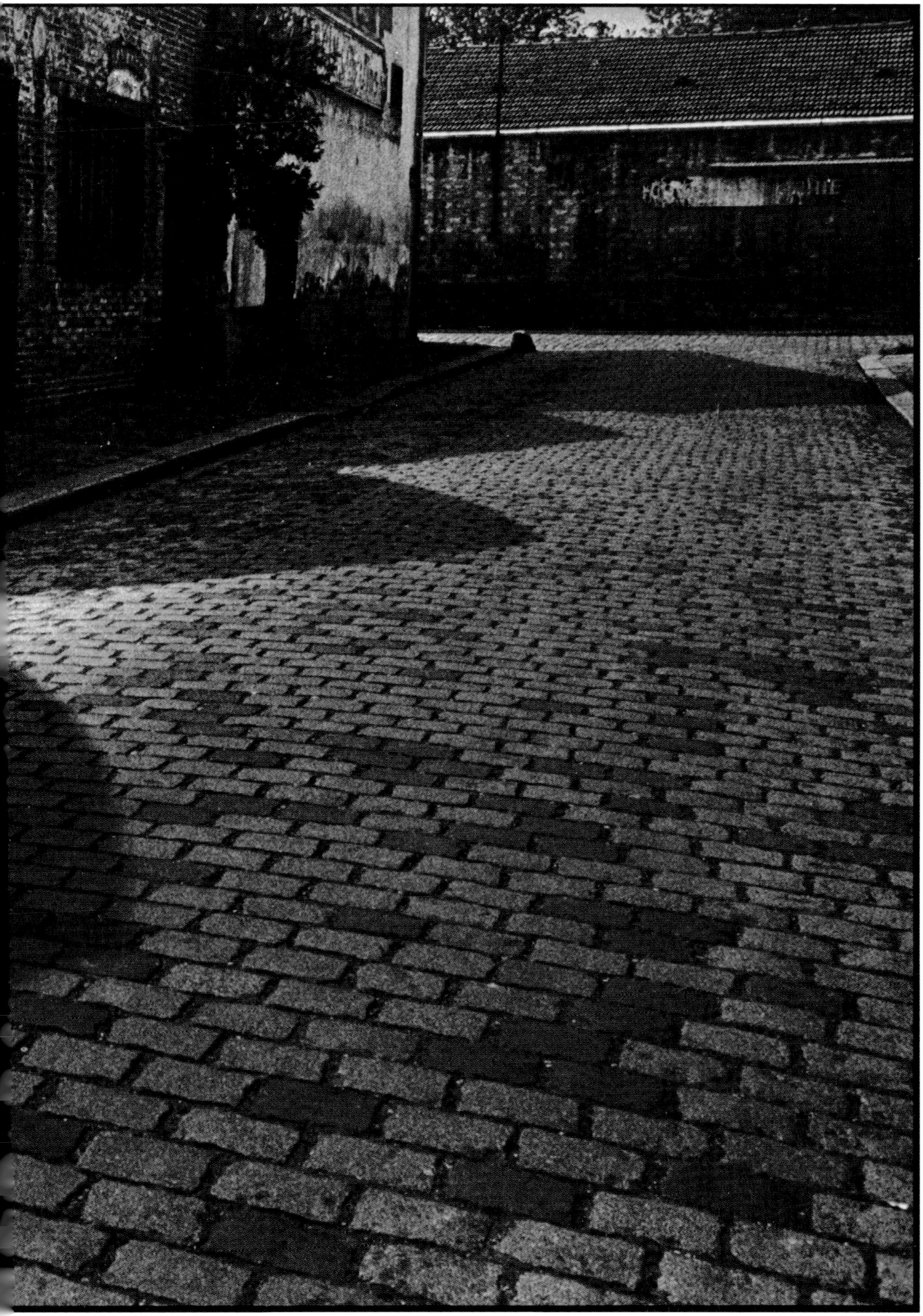

As she was going through the woods, she met with the Wolf, who wanted very much to eat her up. But he dared not do it, because there were hunters who were nearby in the forest. He asked her where she was going. The poor child, who did not know that it was dangerous to stay and talk to a wolf, said to him:

"I am going to see my grandmamma and bring her a custard and a little pot of butter from my mamma."

"Does she live far off?" asked the Wolf.

"Oh! yes," answered Little Red Riding Hood. "It is beyond that mill you see there, at the first house in the village."

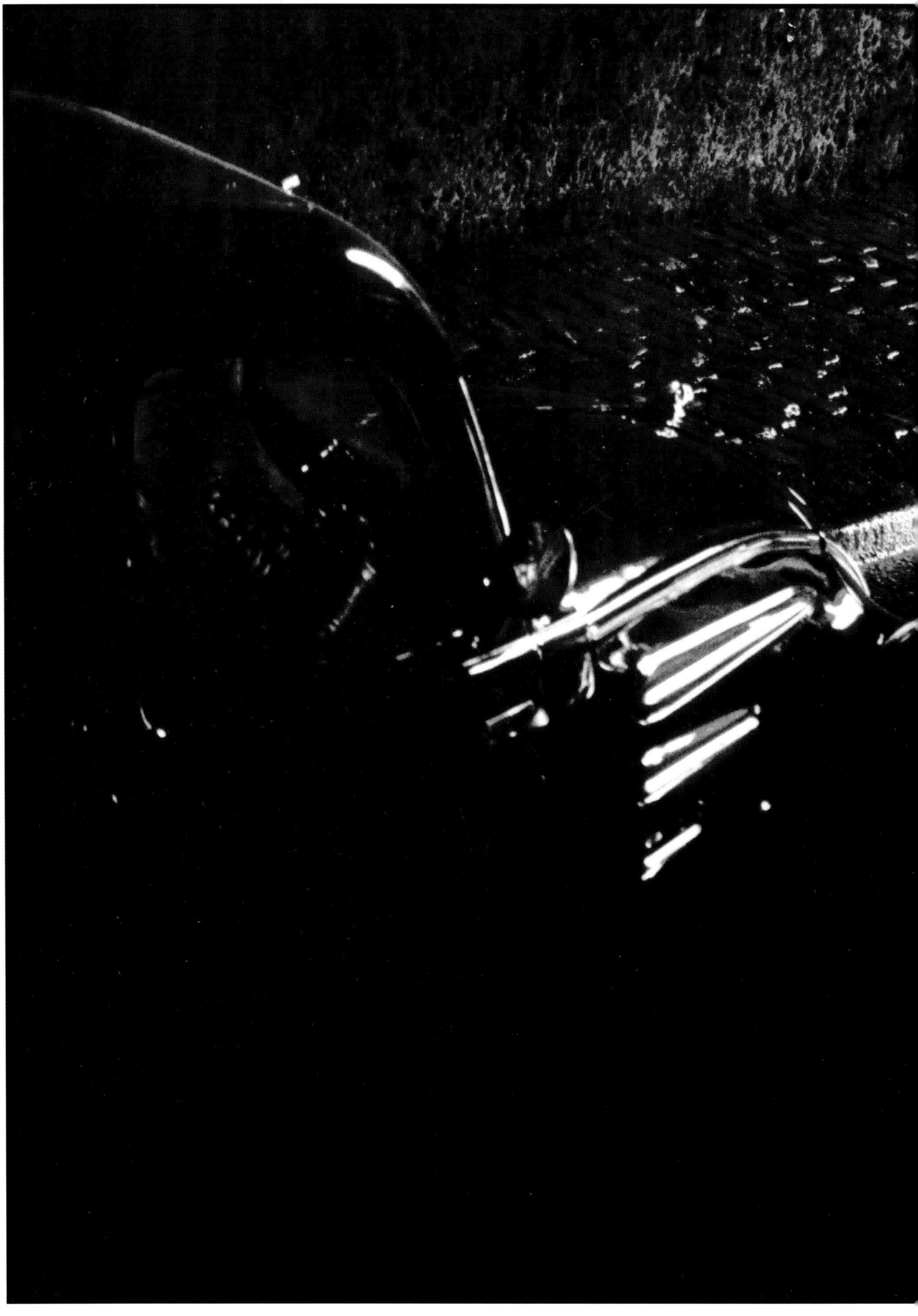

As she was going through the woods, she met with the Wolf.

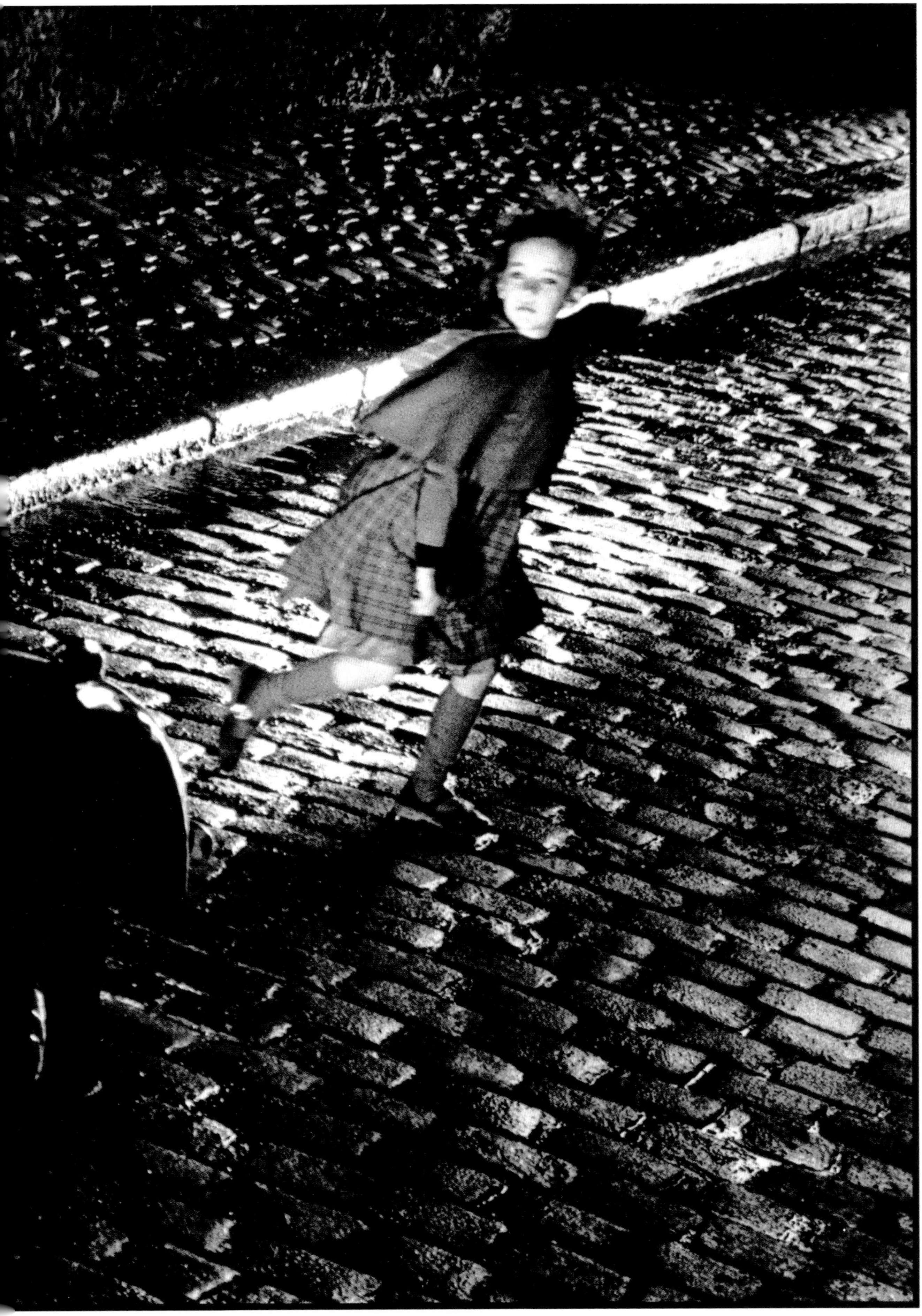

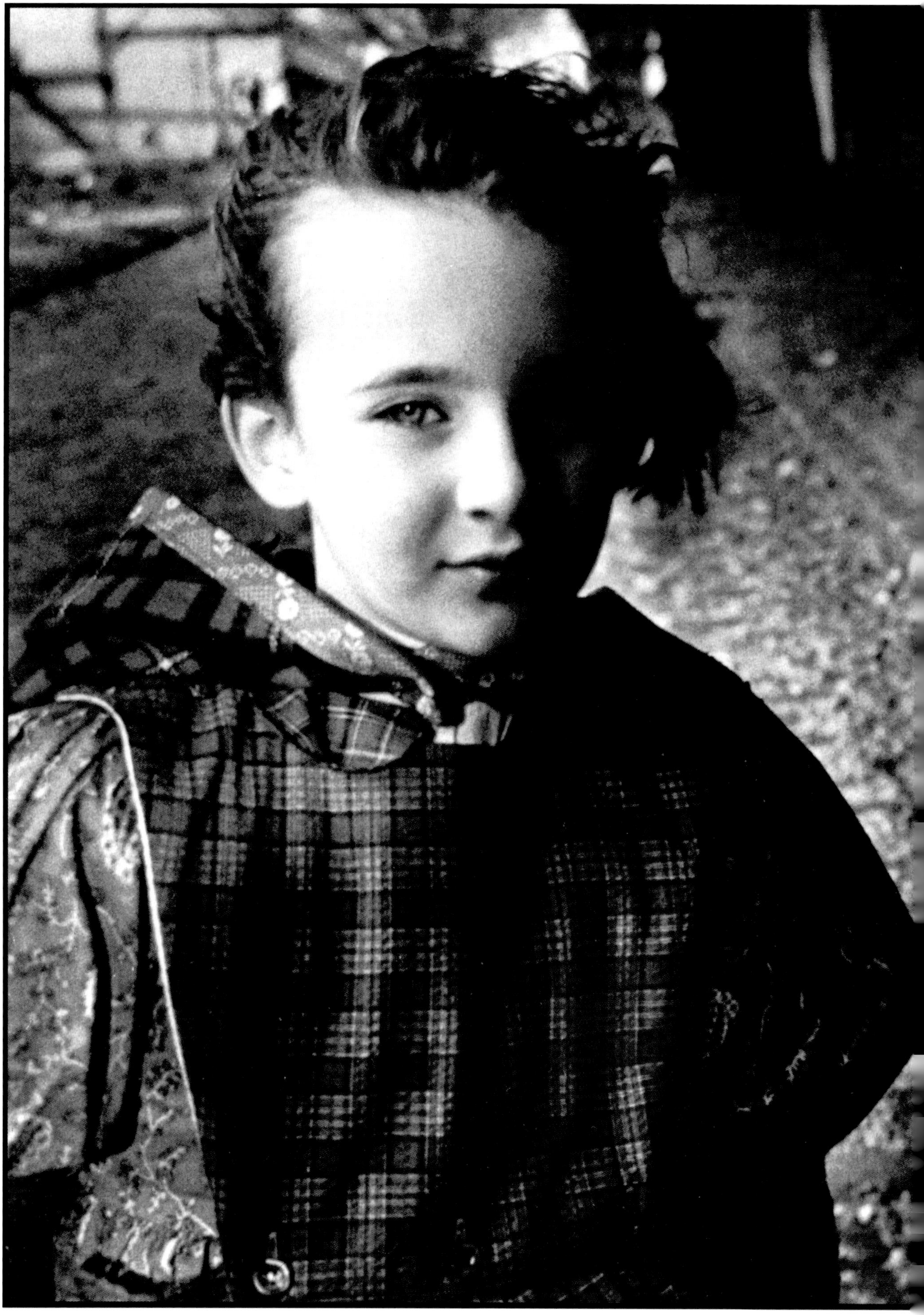

"Does she live far off?" asked the Wolf.

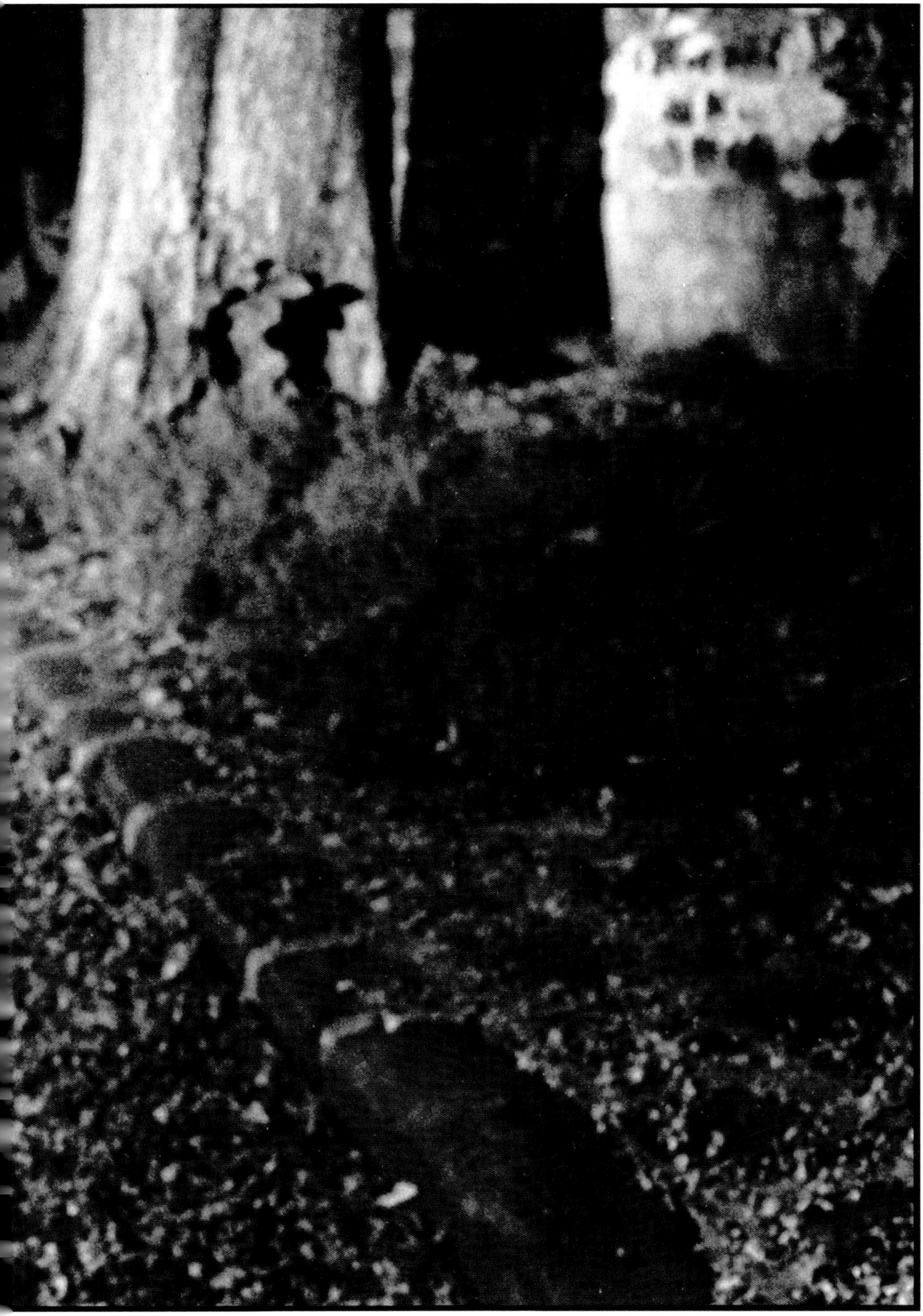

"Oh! yes," answered Little Red Riding Hood. "It is beyond that mill you see there."

"Well," said the Wolf, "I'll go
and see her too. I'll go this way and
you go that way, and we shall see who
will be there soonest."

The Wolf began to run as fast as
he could. He took the short way, and
the little girl went the long way. She
took her time gathering nuts, running
after butterflies, and making bouquets
of the little flowers she saw.

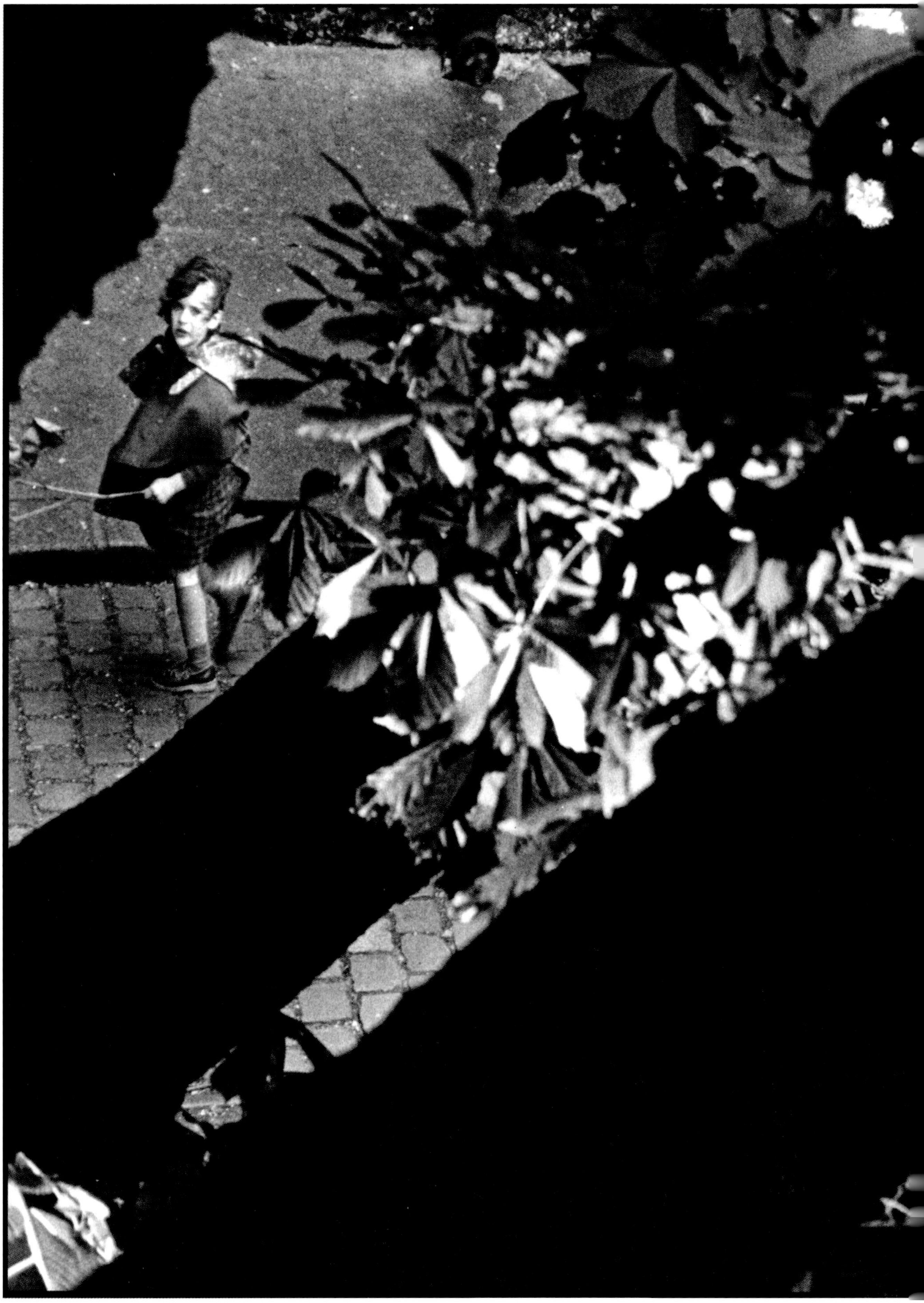

The Wolf began to run as fast as he could. He took the short way, and the little girl went the long way.

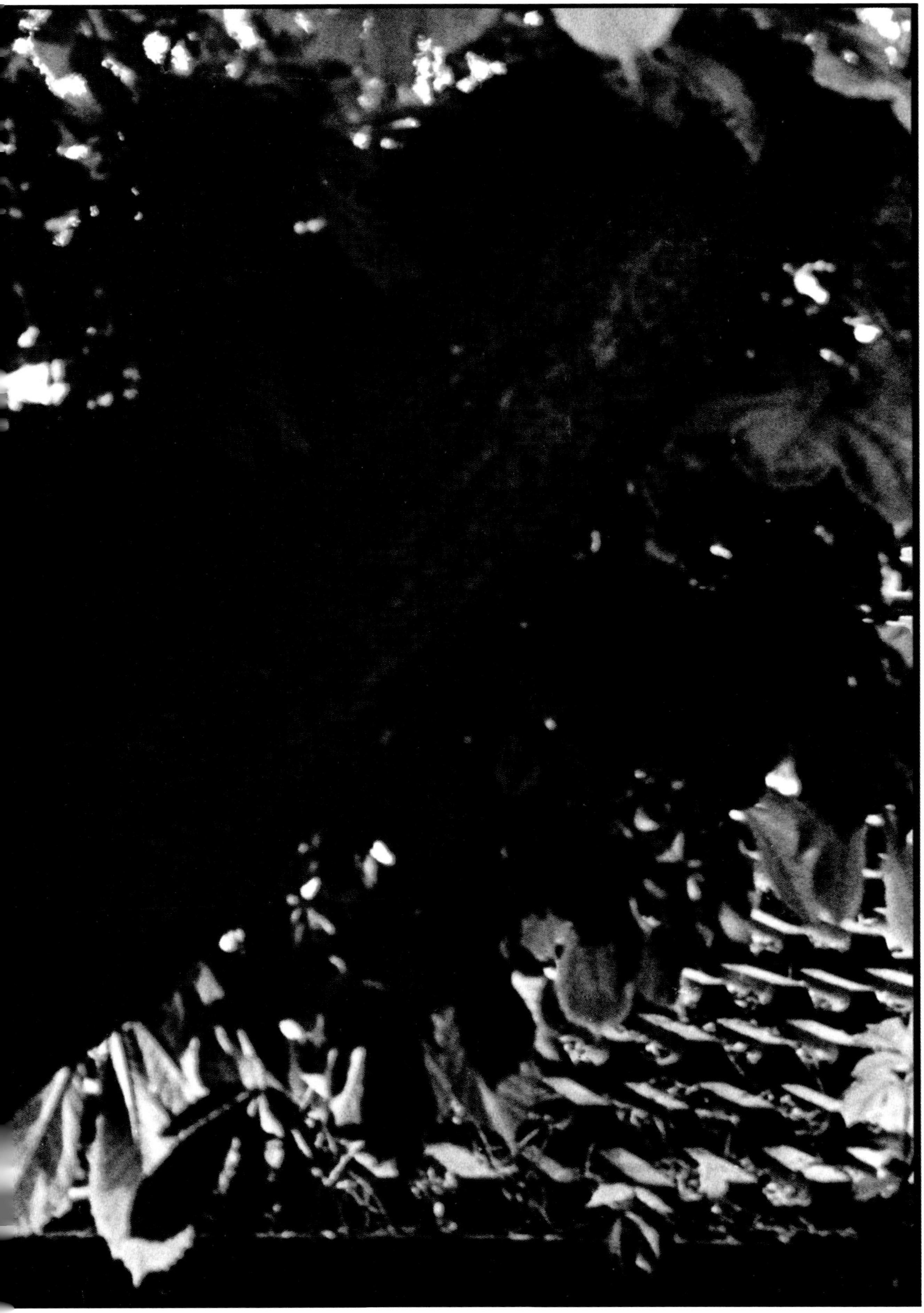

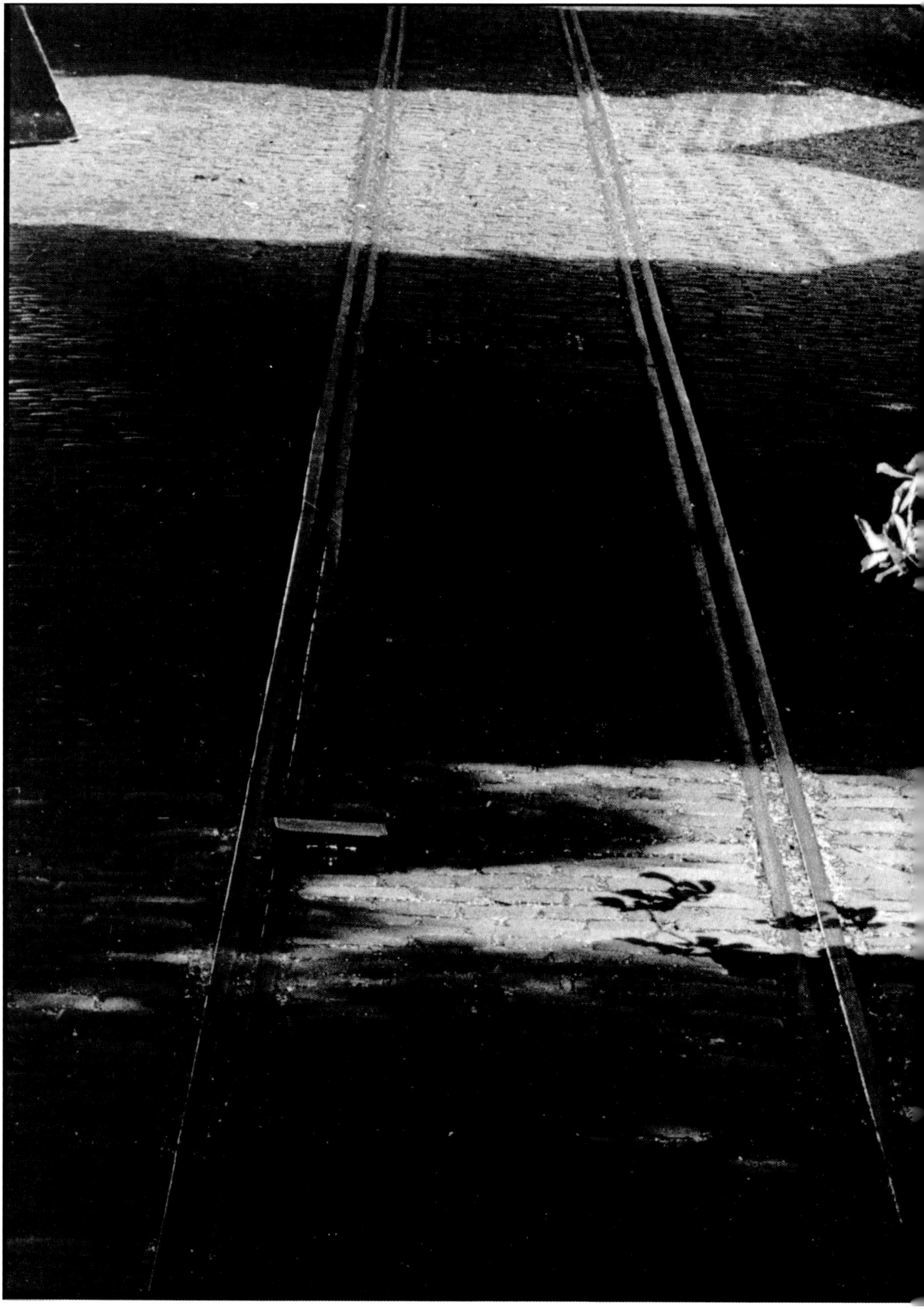

She took her time gathering nuts, running after butterflies, and making bouquets of the little flowers she saw.

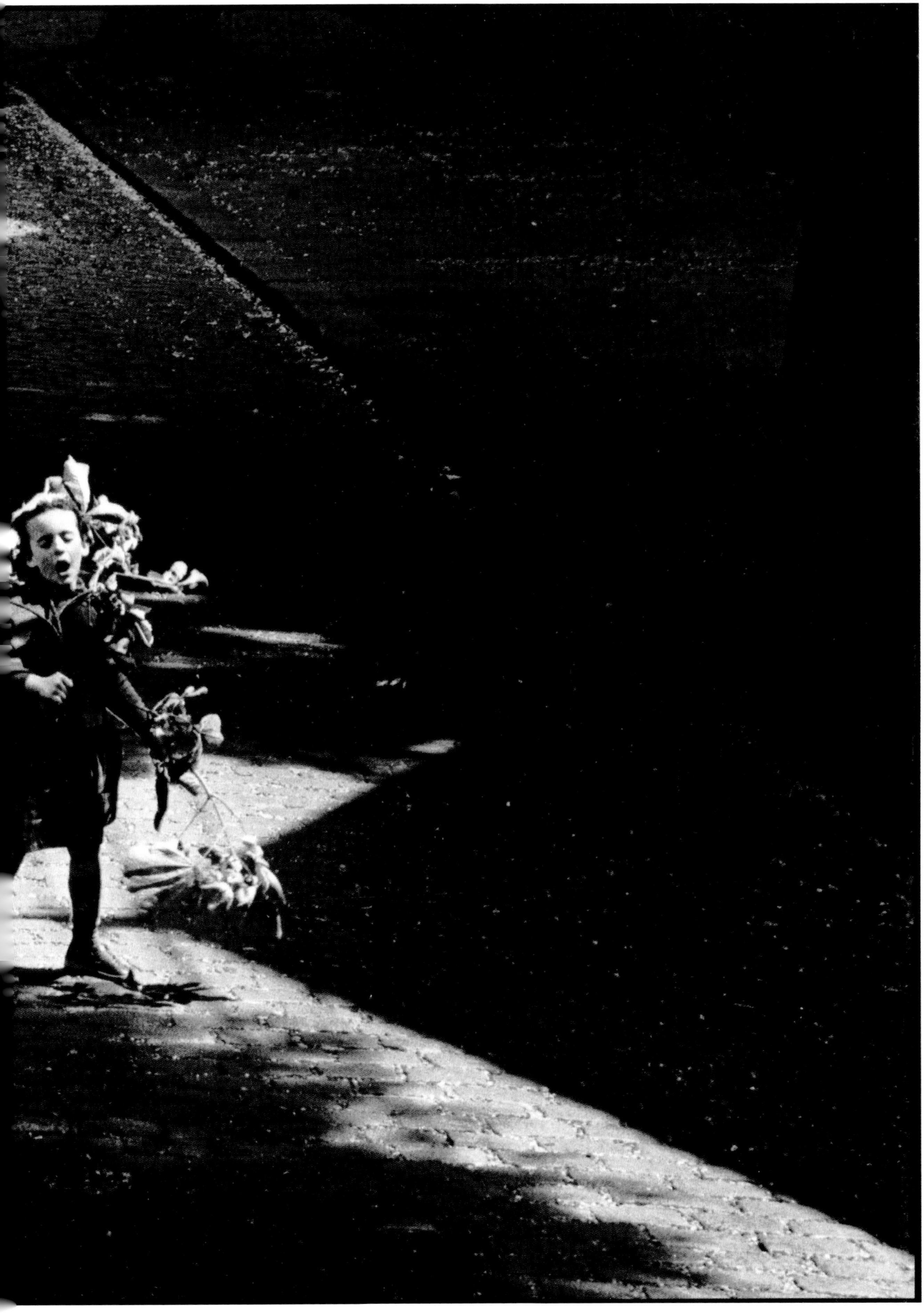

The Wolf quickly arrived at the old woman's house. He knocked at the door—tap, tap.

"Who's there?"

"Your grandchild, Little Red Riding Hood," replied the Wolf, imitating her voice. "I have brought you a custard and a little pot of butter sent by mamma."

The good grandmother, who was in bed because she was somewhat ill, cried out:

"Pull the handle, and the latch will go up."

The Wolf pulled the handle and the door opened. And immediately he fell upon the old woman and ate her up in a moment, for he had not eaten anything in three days.

He then shut the door and got into the grandmother's bed, where he waited for Little Red Riding Hood.

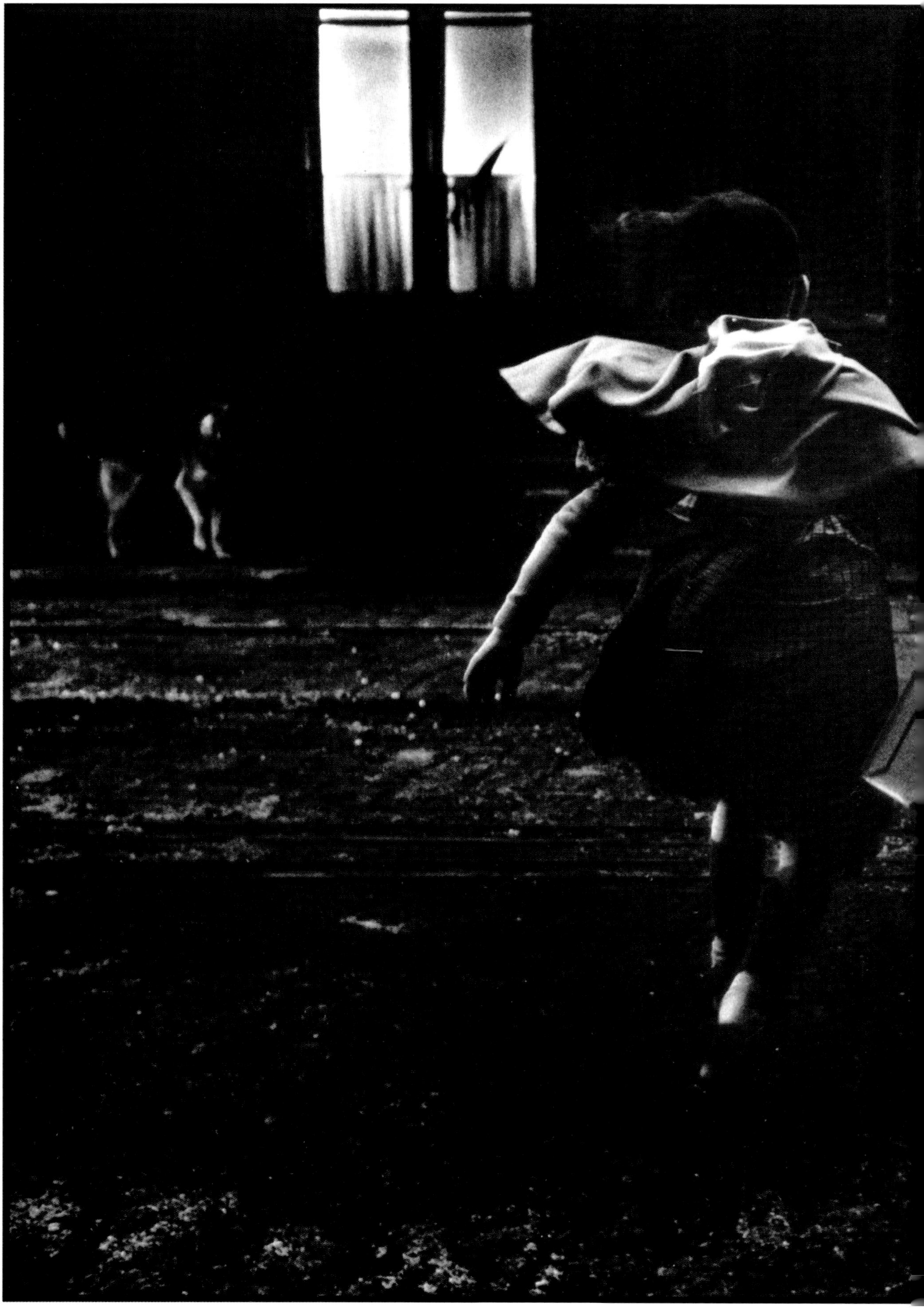

He shut the door and got into the grandmother's bed, where he waited for Little Red Riding Hood.

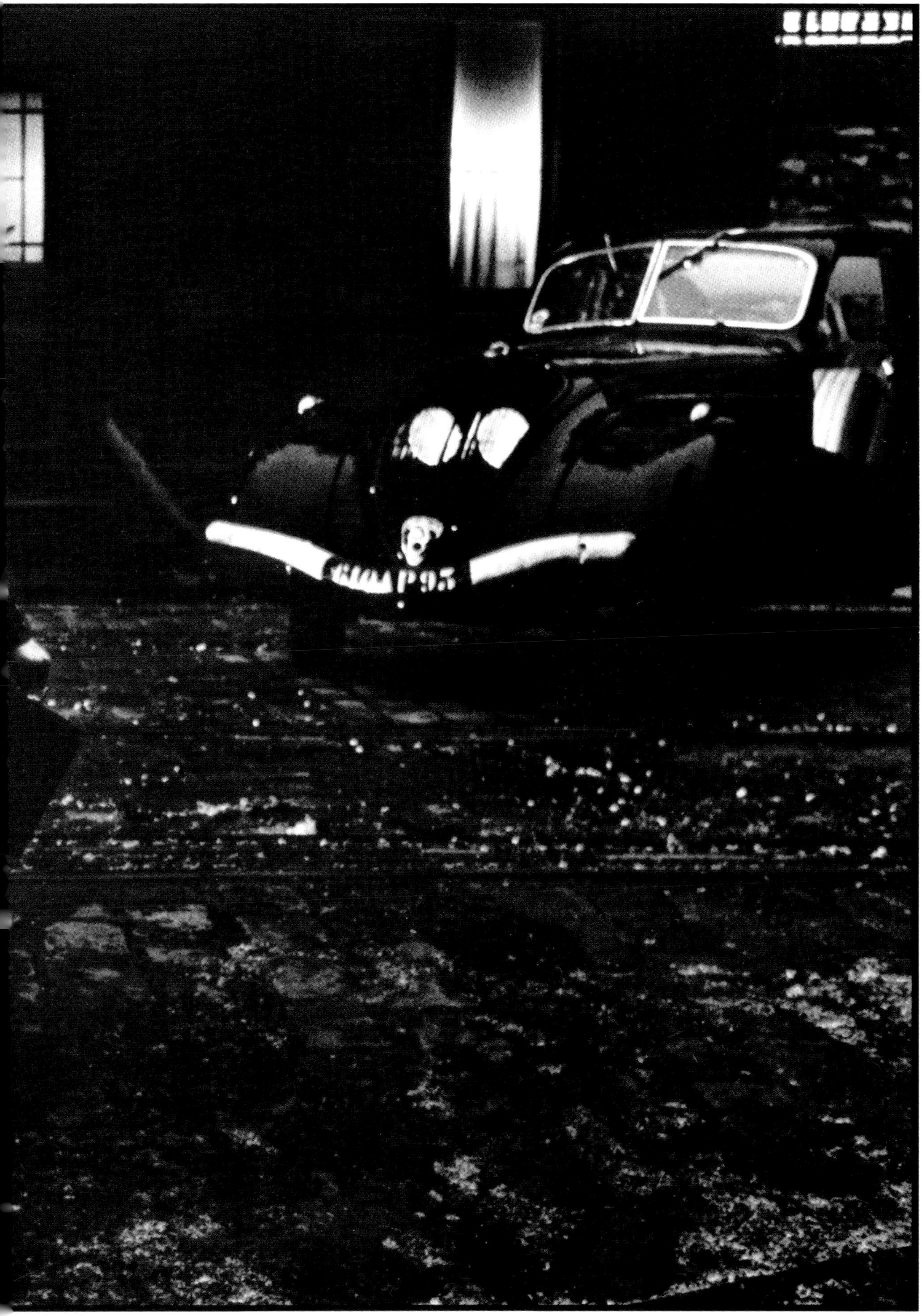

She came some time afterwards and knocked at the door—tap, tap.

"Who's there?"

Little Red Riding Hood, hearing the low voice of the Wolf, was afraid at first. But she believed her grandmother's cold had gotten worse and she was hoarse, so she answered:

"'Tis your grandchild, Little Red Riding Hood, who has brought you a custard and a little pot of butter which mamma sends you."

The Wolf cried out to her, softening his voice as much as he could:

"Pull the handle, and the latch will go up."

Little Red Riding Hood pulled the handle, and the door opened.

The Wolf, seeing her come in, said to her, as he hid under the blankets:

"Put the custard and the little pot of butter on the stool, and come and lie down next to me."

Little Red Riding Hood undressed and climbed into bed.

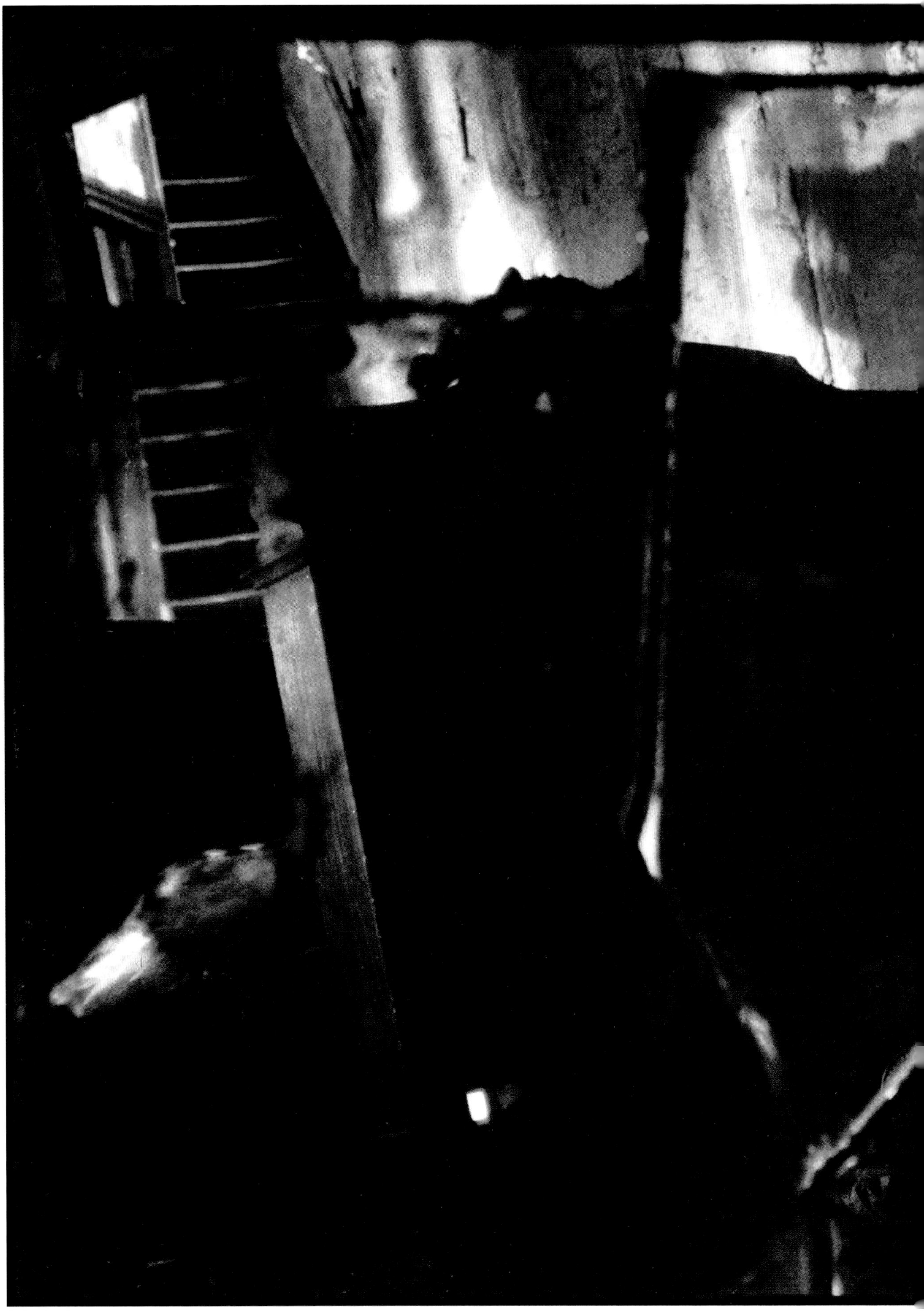

"Put the custard and the little pot of butter on the stool, and come and lie down next to me."

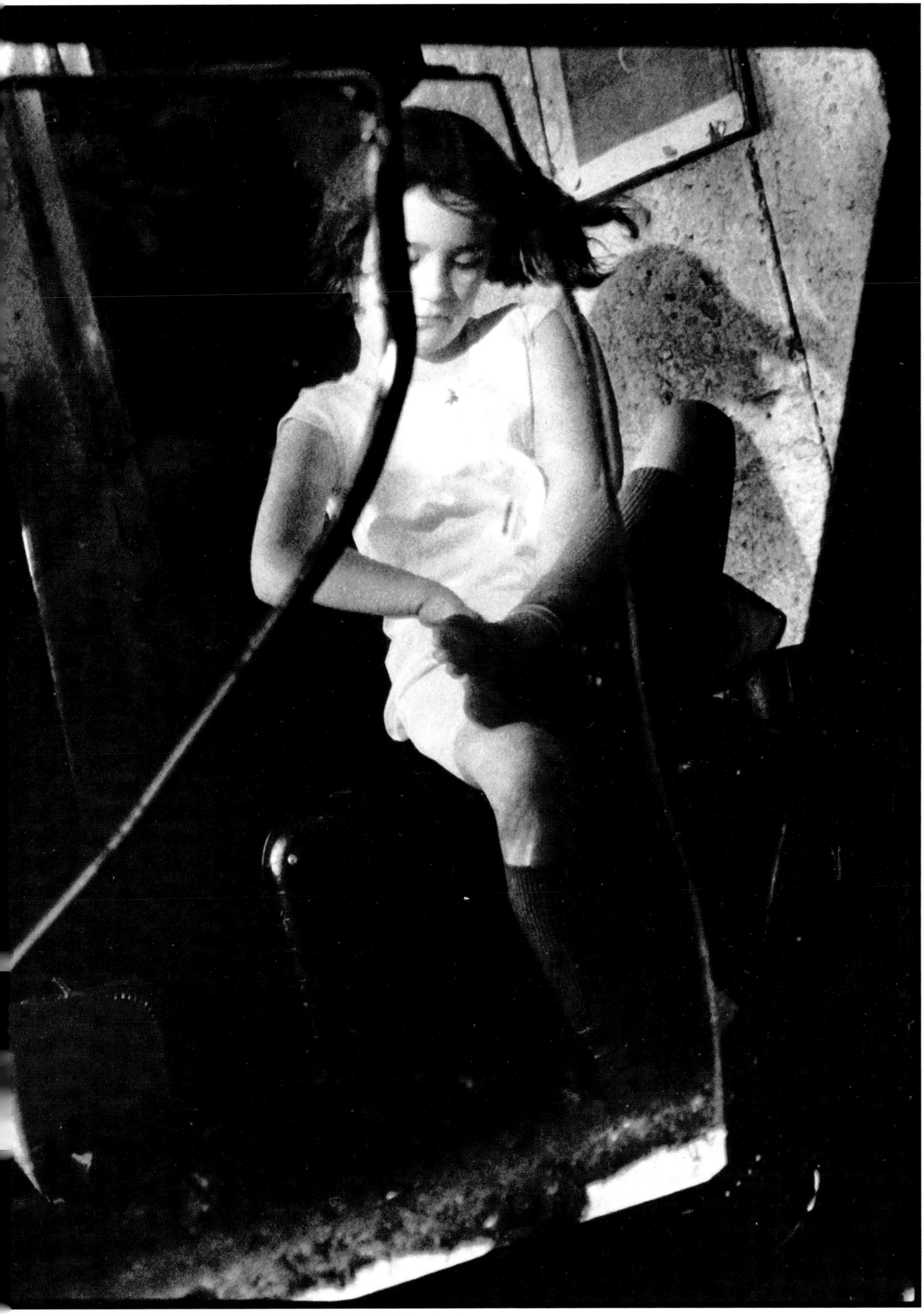

She was greatly amazed to see how her grandmother looked in her nightgown, so she said to her:

"Grandmamma, what big arms you have!"

"The better to hug you with, my dear."

"Grandmamma, what big legs you have!"

"The better to run with, my child."

"Grandmamma, what big ears you have!"

"The better to hear you with, my child."

"Grandmamma, what big eyes you have!"

"The better to see you with, my child."

"Grandmamma, what big teeth you have!"

"The better to eat you up!"

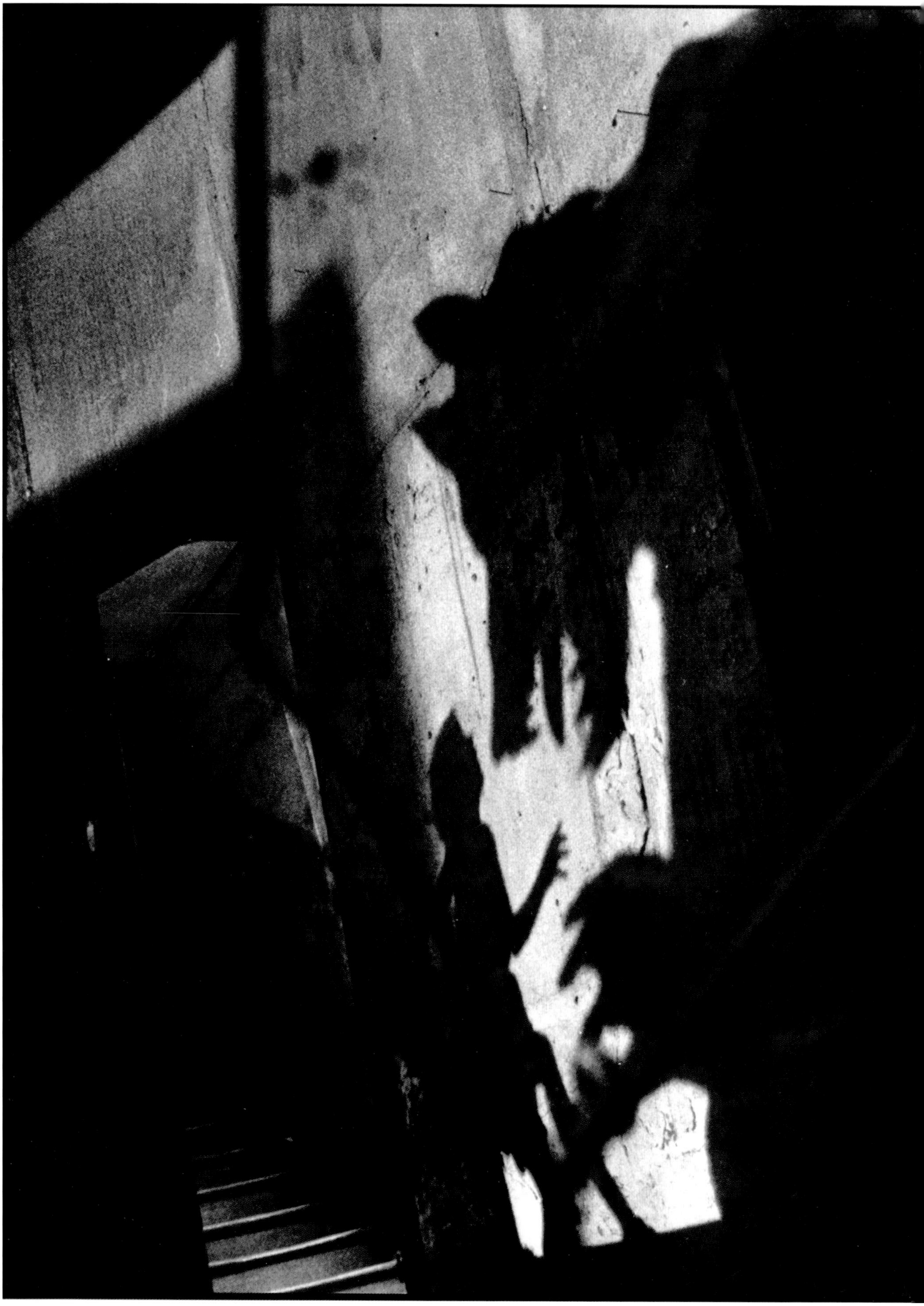

Saying these words, the wicked Wolf fell upon Little Red Riding Hood and ate her up.

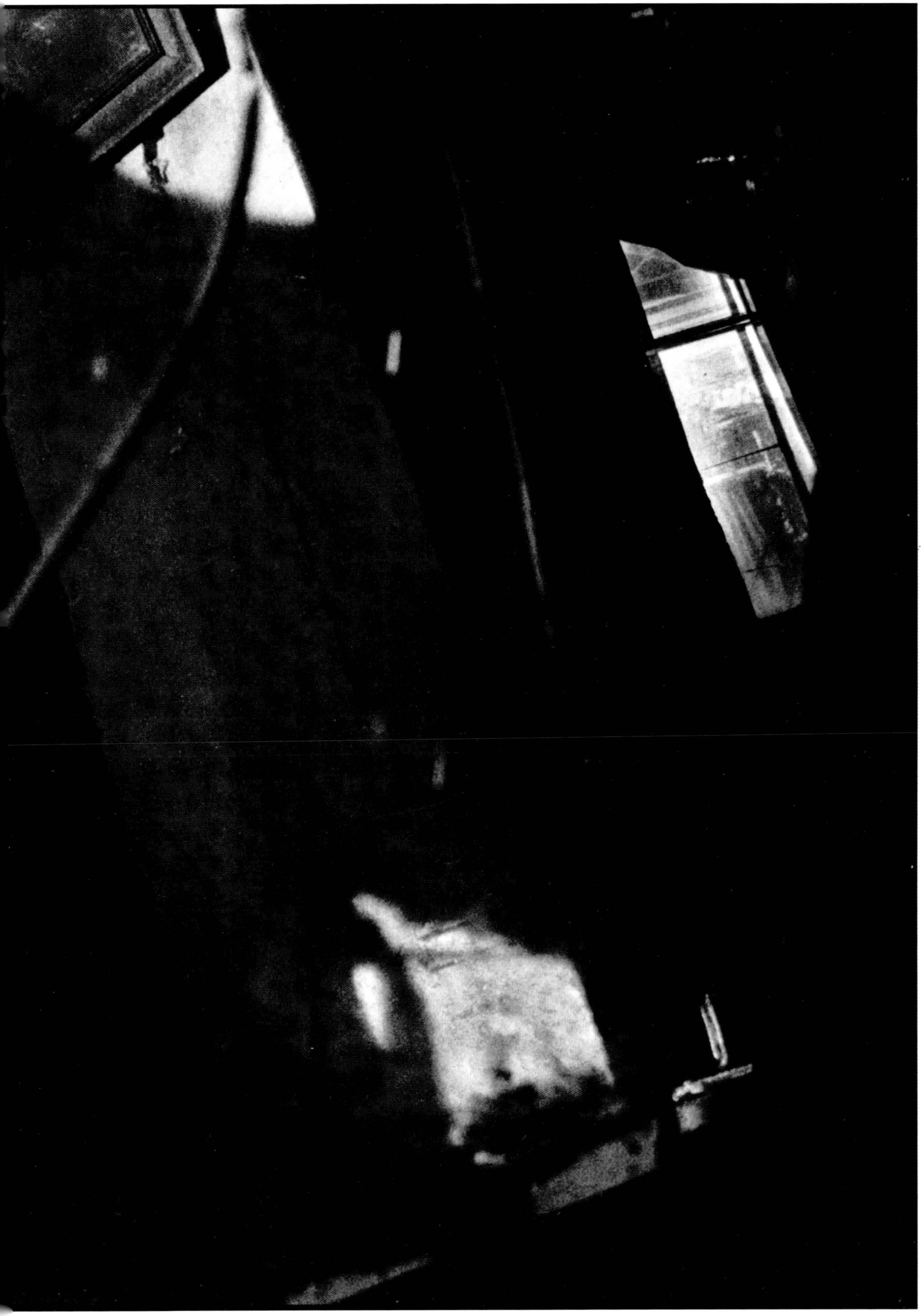

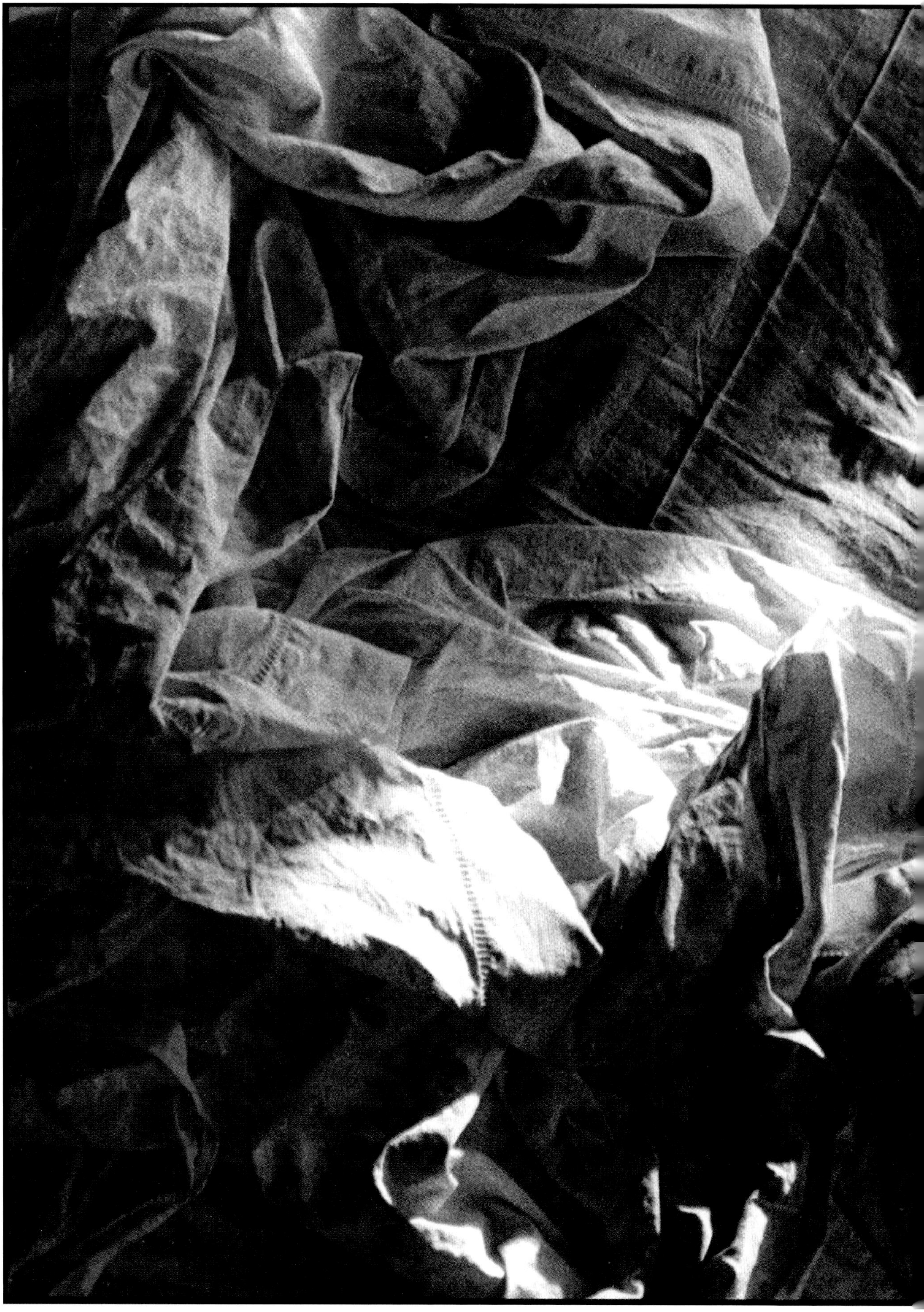

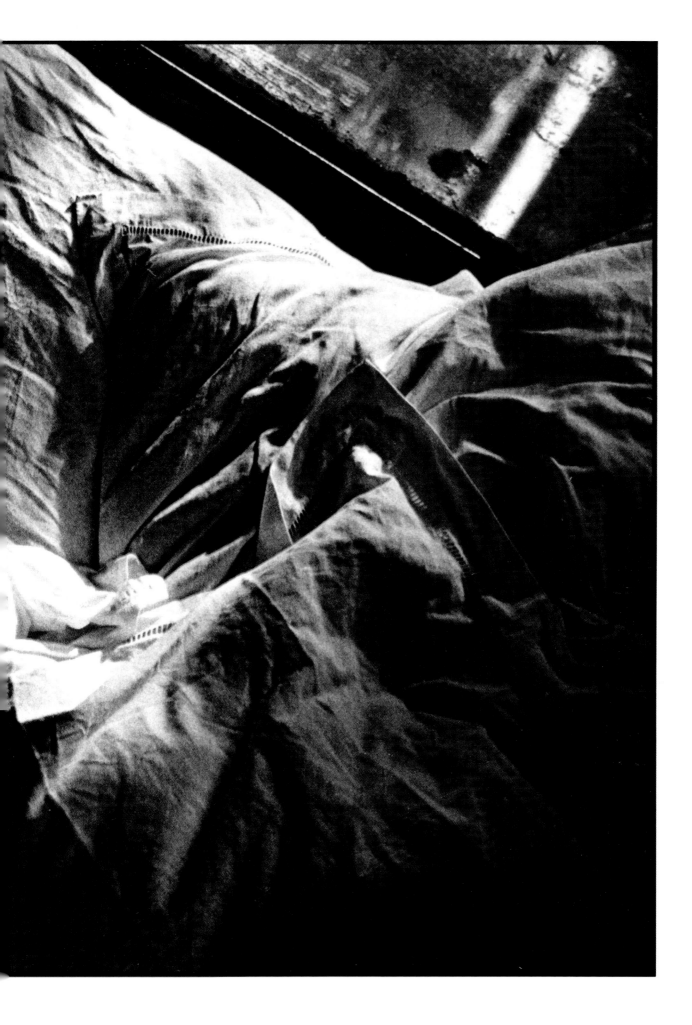

This book was created with the help of Mike Yavel, Aimé Deudé, Florence Lamouche, Emile Ganem, and in collaboration with Bonpoint, Faber Mirolège, and Promobile.